FOR THE LUVVA JACK

A story by
Elliot S! Maggin

CAVEAT CORNER BOOKS

For the Luvva Jack
Copyright © 2017 by Caveat Corner Inc.
All rights reserved.

For the Luvva Jack is a work of fiction.

ISBN-13: 978-1975864200
ISBN-10: 1975864204

For the geeks and the nerds. All of us.
And congratulations on
inventing the Twenty-First Century.

For the Luvva Jack

It was the day after the day after Jack died. You knew Jack. We all knew Jack. I knew him better than I once realized.

My name's Steve. Probably you know me too. I was a few of years short of eighty when Jack died, both of us born in 1917, but I looked about twenty-five. I've looked about twenty-five since I was about twenty-five. I'm an anomaly. I'll get to that.

Jack and I met for what I supposed was the first time just a month or two after I moved out to the west coast. The town was called Thousand Oaks, one of those cookie-cutter suburban housing developments at the molten core of the building boom and people were moving into new homes every few days, it seemed. Jack was a commercial artist, he told me in a voice full of Brooklyn. I helped him and his son carry boxes of books and magazines into the crisp new Cape Cod home that looked suspiciously similar to mine and to every other crisp new home on the block. Jack was a veteran of the Second World War same as I was. He and I both landed at Omaha Beach in France on a Thursday, two days into the initial invasion, and eventually he fought his way deep into the Black Forest in Germany. Turned out we were there at about the same time.

"Comics and book covers," Jack said when I asked him what sort of artwork he did. Actually what he said was probably closer to "bookuvuhs." He said he drew mostly science fiction and action stories."

"You draw them?" I asked him.

"Draw, paint, color in. Acrylics mostly on canvas. Ink on paper. About two or three comic books a month and maybe fifteen or twenty book covers a year."

"Hey I used to spot blacks in an advertising studio. That's real work," I said. "Do you ever come up for air?"

"I work fast," he said.

"A regular Van Gogh, huh?"

"Van Gogh was a piker. What line are you in, Steve?"

"I'm a …" I hadn't settled on a story yet, "… a trainer. Fitness training. I'll be looking for a job with a gym," I made it up on the spot. "But I'm hoping to open a place of my own soon." I made that up too, but it sounded like a pretty good idea.

"You start that business up soon as you can. This town looks to be growing like a whale calf."

"Yeah just look at this neighborhood. I didn't even know your house was completed and here you are. Nobody even put a 'For Sale' sign on it."

"I told you," Jack said, "I work fast."

Thousand Oaks was one of those places that looked at first as though it was airlifted in from the central Ticky-Tack Warehouse, but it turned out to be a nicer spot than anyone expected. It was a suburb to the northwest of Los Angeles. A lot of police and firefighters lived there, and a lot of retired career military folks. There were plenty of schools and scads of good teachers who not only could afford this housing but who also liked living within reach of the big town but away from the rush. There were horse trails and ancient caves with storied pasts. There would always be Starbucks, Old Navy, Barnes & Noble showing up in the crisp new malls, but soon there would be families opening mom-and-pop shops that stuck too. Omelets 'N Things for Sunday brunch. Gloria's Comfortables for prom dresses and graduation suits. Paige's Used Books with a good stock of high school and college texts along with plenty of classic literature and trashy novels. There were young and youngish couples with their growing kids and their tax base, and in the decades Jack and I both lived there the town flourished. It didn't take long before the houses began looking distinct from each other as well, with dormers, extensions, second stories and such. I opened my gym within two or three years – Ye Olde Vigor Shoppe I called it – with my savings and a load of local good will.

Jack had fans, both of his public work and of his private character. It turned out that he was one of the most sought-after illustrators in the world. He painted werewolves and demons for the covers of Stephen King novels, those complex action scenes for the reissue of Robert E. Howard sword-and-sorcery paperbacks that made a resurgence in the eighties, and whenever Sidney Sheldon came out with one of those stories about resilient women in a world full of cruel men Jack whipped out the watercolors and created something sad and sensitive for the paperback release. He loved being around kids and gave free art lessons at the elementary schools in town. He volunteered to design murals for blank walls – the one of the dirt encrusted Wrangler bouncing over a log as it came out of the woods that he painted on the garage at the local Jeep dealership showed up in a national magazine ad. Every Wednesday afternoon for a lot of Wednesdays, sitting on a bench he built himself that circled a black walnut tree out in front of the middle school, he read aloud from his comic books in that raspy east coast cadence. Over the years his audience only grew.

At the funeral I thought maybe we should put a nice plaque on that walnut tree. Maybe we could rename the street after Jack. That was what I was thinking about when the roof tumbled onto the floor of the funeral chapel and the guys in black jumpsuits and grappling ropes showed up.

My plan was to move to a new place every few years to avoid suspicion, but I liked it here. I got in the habit of putting gray streaks in my hair to make it look like I was aging. I tried brushing airplane glue on my forehead and my upper cheeks but I couldn't get it to look like the crow's feet that never managed to show up alongside my eyes. Nobody ever believed these attempts, but they believed in me. People who knew me would rather marvel at the amazing way the hometown fitness guru seemed never to age a day.

I would have been suspicious.

Jack's funeral was at a huge empty expanse of acreage that a big cemetery chain bought not long before and promoted as "the future of the Los Angeles Jewish community," despite my thinking somebody ought to have noticed the irony. In the chapel I couldn't figure out how to keep the yarmulke from falling off my head. Eventually a lady behind me passed up a bobby pin to hold the cap to my hair and I stopped catching it in mid-fall so I could pay more attention. Jack's service started out looking like one of the best funerals I ever attended.

When Jack's grandson Jonathan got up to speak the first thing he said almost apologetically was, "The thing you've got to understand about Grampa is that he just hated Nazis," and everyone in the room practically fell out of their seats laughing. "He just hated Nazis," the grandson said, "whether they show up in board rooms, on talk shows or goose-stepping through the streets of Paris." Every comic book bad guy Jack ever made up seemed to look like some thinly veiled fascist. No one who knew Jack needed to be reminded that in his universe a special corner of Hell was reserved for Nazis.

I had asthma when I was a kid. I was allergic to pretty much everything that walked, grew fur or blew through the air. I was bumped, bullied and terminally measly. The thing was, though, I had a gut level reaction to anyone else being pushed around. If I came across a big kid trying to take advantage of a littler kid I'd step in reflexively and more often than not I'd be the one who got beat up instead of the kid I was defending. I couldn't help myself. I guess that was why in 1942, when I falsified test results to enlist, an army judge advocate gave me a choice between court martial and jockeying a desk stateside for the duration. I told my friends I was running a big mess kit repair base in the Bronx but I really wasn't sure what papers I was shuffling or for what reason. I just made sure the numbers on the bottoms of all the requisition forms added up correctly. After not long, though, I attracted the attention of Wild Bill Donovan.

Colonel Donovan was the guy President Roosevelt appointed to put together an organized intelligence agency to coordinate wartime spying. I thought at first that Donovan wanted to make me a spy but what he really wanted to turn me into was a guinea pig. Despite the fact that we were in the middle of a world war, this was before the era of big federal grants. If you had a few smarts and you wanted to do something memorable you pretty much had to do it on your own, like the Wright brothers. There was a guy in New Mexico fooling around with liquid fueled rockets. He figured out a way to mix liquid oxygen and gasoline and get a tin cylinder he held together with solder to shoot a mile-and-a-half in the sky while the rest of us were still piloting puddle-jumpers. Years later the rocket guy made NASA possible. A doctor from New York had this idea for curing polio. He put together a club of 20-thousand medical folks and nearly as many public schools up and down the east coast and vaccinated a quarter-million kids and not a single one of those kids contracted polio in the next few years. Considering the illness was one of the biggest kid-killers abroad in the land that was statistically impossible unless the thing was working. It was the closest thing I've ever seen to proving a negative. When someone asked this doctor how much his vaccine cost he said, "There is no patent. Could you patent the sun?" That was the way a lot of people talked in those days.

So Wild Bill got wind of another scientist who thought he could single-handedly wipe out the Nazis. This guy – I called him the Old Doc – had advanced degrees and an ace rep and a government at war just didn't ignore guys like that. The Old Doc wrote up a proposal that crossed Donovan's desk. It had diagrams and charts explaining why he needed a pile of bucks from the OSS – FDR's new spy agency – and an elaborate lab setup and he could create an army of super soldiers. The Colonel, never one to buy a pig in a poke, promptly burned the proposal, told the Doc to destroy any copies he had, and Donovan said he wanted to see the thing work. Wild Bill figured the thing to do was find a skinny, physically powerless, headstrong kid, maybe one with a surfeit of patriotism, and plug him in. When he came across the file on me he thought he'd hit the mother lode.

The doctor had an assistant he called Osprey. He was a short stocky guy around my age who did most of the heavy lifting. Donovan had rescued me from my desk job and put me through a flurry of medical tests of one sort or other. Blood. Fluoroscopy. Neuro. That kind of thing.

One evening, at a time the colonel instructed, I swallowed as much spaghetti and beer as I could hold down – raw material – and the next day I went to the facility Donovan had made possible. It was in a little corner of Greenpoint on the shore of the East River. I found Osprey running around lifting things and assembling things and setting dials and running up to me with a tape measure and quantifying things, and there was the Old Doc perched on a platform behind his big mechanism. The Doc issued orders at Osprey, loud and quick like a carnival barker. He had a kind of newswire setup on a desk that kept clackety-clacking out pages of data about my blood work or about the numbers Osprey fed him.

"Hold up your left arm please, pal?" Osprey requested.

I complied and he measured the distance from my armpit to the tip of my thumb. He wound his tape measure around my bicep, such as it was. He wrote things down – presumably the measurements he came up with – in a composition book.

"Open your mouth please?" He pulled a wooden tongue depressor out of a shirt pocket but instead of looking down my throat he used it to scrape on my inner cheek. Then he put the tongue depressor in a metal box on a table near the doc's platform.

Osprey yelled up at the Doc every time he measured something or looked at a dial or at the level of multicolor fluids in a long rank of narrow tubes, about bacteria cultures on my skin scrapings, about atmospheric conditions, about phases of the Moon or sunspot activity for all I know.

"Readings appear consistent with the subject's identifiers," the Doc called down after a few minutes.

I stood around that big converted warehouse with those two guys treating me like a lab rat for over half an hour before Wild Bill Donovan showed up – in full military regalia with epaulets and a scrum of medals on his chest and pleats in his pants. He wore a sword on his belt and tucked a riding crop under his arm. Before, he had always seemed to have a camouflage of dust and disorder around him, but this was the first time I had seen him in uniform. He looked spiffy as an explorer scout. With a sidearm and a sword for pity's sake.

"How're you feeling, kid?" he asked, standing ramrod straight gazing at a far wall. Seemed he was posing for … what? A statue? A stamp? "Kid?" he asked after a moment.

"You mean me, Colonel?"

"Who else would I be talking to? Are you okay today?"

"Uhh," I said. I was still stuffed with carbs from last night's binge. Then, "Yeah. I'm fine."

"Terrific. It's good to be fine."

I noticed for the first time that the doc had stopped barking and Osprey had stopped scurrying the moment the colonel walked in. The younger man still feverishly assembled stuff, putting things on top of things, fitting things into other things, and the Old Doc studied data, deep in thought, but neither made a peep any more. Clearly there was some sort of pecking order here but I had no idea whether or where I fit into it.

Osprey was still assembling his mechanism when Donovan said, "You ready to do this thing?"

"Sure," I said and laughed. "Today? Now?"

"Uh-huh," from the colonel.

"Yeah, I'm all for physiological transformation before lunch. And then we can go take over the Rhineland."

"Maybe we'll save that for next week. Today it's just the treatment and then we head south. There's a 'copter waiting at Idlewild."

I seriously thought he was kidding. But Osprey said "Ready to go" and Wild Bill led me to a copper cylinder in the middle of the mechanism Osprey was assembling. The cylinder was the size of a big man, a man much bigger than I was. Osprey held it open on a kind of hinged apparatus.

"Aren't you going to test it with a gerbil or something?"

"We've run enough tests. There's a war on. This has to be broken down and moved as soon as we're done. Up you go. Unless you're having sudden second thoughts."

After what I thought might have been a moment too much hesitation I said, "Not a chance," and stepped into the big cylinder. Osprey fastened a leather belt loosely across my chest and another one below my waist. The Doc appeared to my left with a hypodermic the size of a water tumbler, filled with a liquid that glowed like a fluorescent bulb. I don't remember anything that happened after that.

Jack pulled at somewhere in my memory from the minute I first met him. Rather, that is when I thought I first met him. I think I ultimately recognized him by his voice. He was a lot older and thicker now, but he walked the same way. His accent was the same although his voice was deeper and much rougher. The second time I came across him – it was two days after I first helped him and his son carry boxes into their new house – I looked at his eyes. The eyes made it easier.

Jack was Osprey, the doc's assistant who measured and poked at me so much that day. I never brought it up. But I knew.

I didn't have to wonder what he was doing here in the suburbs, raising a family. He was my signal that the powers that be knew where I was, but I wondered what his specific orders were. I thought of leaving, of disappearing again, but I never did. At least here I knew who was watching me.

I suppose they ran some sort of charge or something through my body in that copper chamber; I wouldn't know. The first sensation I could remember after the doc injected me with his potion – it was a couple of hours ago now – was an ache deep in every muscle in my body, and desperate nausea. It didn't help that besides feeling the upward flood of vomit from my gut, I smelled it too. I forced my eyes open and realized what I was smelling was all over my front shirt. I didn't recognize that shirt, but it seemed big. I was studying it, wondering how it could be that I was filling the big thing up, when I realized that I was several hundred feet above the ground.

I was in something like a helicopter, only bigger. I had never seen one before that didn't have a bubble front, but this one was a small room beating through the sky. I tried to say something but I couldn't hear myself over the noise and I couldn't feel my words through the tight crowded feeling in my throat. Someone clapped a speaker mechanism over my mouth and phones over my ears. I looked to my left and saw that it was Colonel Donovan who sat next to me, strapped in a seat and still in full dress blues.

I managed to get a word out. "Where?" I croaked.

"Going to see the boss, kid," Donovan's tinny voice came through the earphones. "Southern Pennsylvania at the moment. You woke up just in time. See that long building down there?"

I looked out the window. I was probably airsick.

"That's where they make Hershey Bars," Donovan said and pointed.

The rising airsickness vanished like a breeze when I realized I was ravenously hungry. "Food?" I wanted to know.

"Whuzzat?" the tinny voice said.

"Chocolate," I said. A candy bar would be a godsend, I thought.

"Get the kid some of that shit-in-a-straw," Wild Bill said into his mouthpiece, apparently to someone behind us.

From back there, someone handed me a glass milk bottle filled with something green and almost liquid, with a fat paper straw sticking out the top. I looked at it for a moment, then shoved the mouthpiece below my chin and sucked out the contents of the bottle without bothering to taste it.

"More," I said, forgetting that I didn't have the speaker on and nobody could hear me. Donovan passed me another quart bottle of the stuff anyway and took the empty one. I drank this slowly enough to notice its texture if not its taste. It was kind of soupy, kind of gravelly – harsh but not unpleasant, and it was beginning to cure my hunger and thirst. By my fourth quartful I began to notice the taste, like ground broccoli. I had never liked broccoli before, but today I liked it fine.

I closed my eyes and felt my body start to feel better. I must have fallen back asleep because when I looked again we were on the ground, in the middle of a big green lawn surrounded by forest. A collection of wooden cabins gathered at a far end of the clearing. About a dozen men, some in suits, some in naval uniforms, ran toward the helicopter from the direction of the cabins.

"Get on up, Stevie-Kid," Wild Bill jostled me and unclipped my seat straps. "Look at you. You're looking more normal already."

I stretched my arms and legs and did look at myself. I didn't look like myself at all. I thought I looked better. I had gone to sleep a skinny kid and now I was – what? – fat. But in my body now, gallons of carbohydrates furiously engaged with tissue and chemicals to construct dense muscles and to harden my bones.

"You were quite the tub o' lard a couple hours ago when we loaded you in this rig," Colonel Donovan said, trying to help me out of the 'copter but nearly tripping himself up on the damn sword. Two uniformed seamen helped me down.

"Where are we now?" I asked.

"The boss calls it Shangri-La. This way. This way."

I could move better now. In fact it felt good to move. As we approached the largest of the cabins, flanked by seamen and dangerous looking guys in suits, a door of the cabin opened and a man pushed a wheelchair from the door down a ramp to the lawn. In the chair was a man clutching a blanket over his legs.

In a few more steps, my eyes focusing, I realized that the man in the chair grinning ear to ear was the president of the United States.

"As you were, Colonel," Franklin Roosevelt said. "Is this our super-soldier?"

That was the last time I let much of anything take me by surprise.

✪   ✪   ✪

I daydreamed at the funeral service but I was vaguely aware of the beating of rotors somewhere nearby. I had no doubt it was the local police, who just loved their aerial reconnaissance vehicles. They kept two helicopters in the air somewhere above Ventura County at all times. No one thought anything of it, other than Jack's grandson Jonathan who had to continue his eulogy a bit louder for a moment.

Then the ceiling thirty-something feet above the funeral chapel cracked in an irregular webbed pattern radiating outward from a point above the stage area behind Jack's simple pine coffin. That was where the shards of the ceiling and the roof above tumbled with a crash in dozens of pieces. Jack's young eulogist managed to step away but he got caught in the cloud of dust as four men in black jumpsuits and masks slid down ropes they looped under all four corners of the coffin and the helicopter above the building hoisted it upward.

All four men yanked sidearms from their waists as two rode the coffin up through the hole in the roof. One man remained on the stage, holding open the back door of the chapel with one hand and brandishing his pistol in the other. The fourth ran up the center aisle of the chapel and out the main door through which we had all come in. By the time the last man did that, however, I was already out the door among a few dozen other outdoor attendees – the overflow crowd – who sat on folding chairs listening to the service.

Perhaps twenty-five or thirty seconds elapsed by now since the cracks first appeared in the chapel ceiling. It didn't make much sense for me to try to follow the coffin up through the hole in the roof, not with armed men guarding against such an eventuality. But it was reasonable to suppose that the two whose job it was to make sure the attendees stayed out of the way had another escape route. When the man in black appeared out the front door brandishing his gun I was sitting in one of the outside chairs near the front of the patio, trying to look as though I had been sitting there the whole time. My jacket and tie were already off, draped over the back of my chair.

When the man scooted by me, among the collection of variously confused, oblivious or intimidated overflow attendees, I stood up behind him. I grabbed the gun hand – his left – and simultaneously clapped my other hand over his face. He was prepared, in principle, for some resistance. He was not prepared for me.

Using his nose as a handle, I pulled his face to the right and with my thumb under the wrist of his left hand I twisted downward on the hand that held the gun as though it were a chicken leg and I felt a crack.

He was strong. I didn't quite remove the hand from his wrist but it would not be picking anything up for a long time. The gun clattered to the ground.

As I mashed the man's face onto the concrete walkway I swept his weapon off the ground and tossed it behind me into a planter by the chapel door.

Somewhere in front of me a big man among the attendees stood from his chair, set his eyes and assumed the posture. He held his head back and his chin up, let his right arm dangle by his side and pointed toward me with his left, about to say something. He was a police officer. They're easy to recognize.

Before he could speak I told him, "The pistol is in the planter. Get it out of here and have it dusted." I've always found that guys who are used to obeying orders will reflexively take orders from me.

"Willco," he said after a moment. He really said that. By now I had Jack's assailant stripped down to his underwear.

"Do you have cuffs?" I asked the policeman.

"I have plastic ties," and he produced a few from a pocket.

"Good enough." I had the man's black shirt on over my own and I poured myself into his trousers. I yanked off his cowl and mask and held them in my hand as I said, "Get him processed."

I got the mask and hood over my head just as the beating of the 'copter got louder and the craft appeared from over the building. It was an oversize black Marine-style Huey the size of a blue whale.

A nylon line with a loop at the end dropped from the craft and I grabbed at it, stepped in the loop and I was out of there.

✪   ✪   ✪

When I finished bulking up and hardening down I had what seemed – at least to me – to be inhuman strength and stepped-up senses. It took only a matter of hours for me to transform. Right away I could tell when a place smelled wrong. I could tell there was infra-red heat or ultra-violet radiation in a room, although I couldn't see it. I was fast, I was strong and durable and I was rarely tired out by anything. I could read upside down as easily as rightside up and I surmised a lot of classified information that way. I knew from a trace of ash in the air the last time I saw him, that President Roosevelt would be dying soon. I felt odd that it was so obvious to me, because nobody else around him seemed to know.

"Are you getting enough sleep, sir?" I asked him during that meeting in his office. I think he heard me but he ignored the question.

Wild Bill was there. The president had made him a general not long after my transformation, and he gave me the rank of captain without specifying what branch of the service I represented. I reported to the president. There were two other military types in that meeting, both chiefs of staff, and I had seen Osprey sitting in the anteroom opposite the president's secretary when I was on my way in. I had not seen the lab assistant since the day of my transformation and I wasn't sure he would recognize me now.

"Hi," I said. "How're you doing?"

"Been better," Osprey said.

"Yeah? How's the Old Doc?"

"They didn't tell you?" the young lab assistant said. "Gone."

"Excuse me?" I looked at him, but General Donovan came in the room behind me and shoved me into the Oval before I could get a question out or an answer back.

"Later for that, Steve," Wild Bill said and the army chief of staff clapped the door shut as soon as we were inside.

Usually I would get my orders by a secure teletype line and I would just go. Sometimes someone would show up at my apartment in Silver Spring or, later on, at the pied à terre they got me in Antwerp and hand me a file folder and I was gone within a few minutes. I had an interesting war. I had been places and seen and done things I would never tell anyone about. Today, though, it seemed they were actually letting me in on the decision-making.

"We've got a situation, gentlemen," the president began. "What do you know about radioactivity, Steve?"

"Radioactivity sir? Almost nothing."

"You're going to have to get smart about it fast," Roosevelt said. "I had to. I had to read a couple of books and technical monographs by people who know things I'll still never understand. I had to do this just to grasp the implications of a letter I got from Doctor Einstein a few years ago. It scared the juice out of me and the information you're getting today is going to scare even the likes of you. Only the men in this room and some scientists working at an isolated location know what we're about to explain to you. You'll be on a plane back to Europe this afternoon and you'll have lots to read on the way."

Then Franklin Roosevelt and the three generals in the room told me about the Manhattan Project.

For five years now – longer than America had been in the war – a small team of engineers and applied physicists had been working on what later came to be known as the atomic bomb. Donovan and his boys recently confirmed that the Germans had a similar program in the works. My job would be to find out how far along the enemy's research had gone and, if possible, intercept and abort shipments of uranium to a German town called Hechingen in the Black Forest.

"Which atomic weight?" I asked the Air Corps chief of staff during my White House briefing.

"Which what?" the general said.

"Uranium-238 or some isotope?" I wanted to know. It was a very heavy element and it was reasonable to suppose they were looking for a highly radioactive iteration of it.

The general hesitated a moment and President Roosevelt said, "It looks like 235 is the most fissile version of the stuff. We find uranium ore in granite quarries. It shows up as dark streaks in the rocks. Our men are synthesizing it using a variety of weight-separation processes. It'll all be in your briefing papers, Captain." The president glanced at the Air Corps chief of staff and said, "Should have been in yours too, General."

The plan was that in Hechingen I would pose as a medical student from Switzerland on a research fellowship at a nearby hospital, and make friends with a guy named Werner Heisenberg. His name was familiar to me but I had to look up the intel on him. He headed the German team developing the bomb. Calling myself Swiss was an attempt to cover for the fact that my German accent was not very good. I just hoped Heisenberg wasn't smart enough to know the difference between German with a Swiss accent and with an American accent. Heisenberg turned out to be plenty smart.

Meanwhile, Osprey had a more dangerous assignment than I did.

✪   ✪   ✪

It didn't even take long enough for me to get the mask off my head before the guys in the 'copter realized I wasn't the guy they left behind. The twenty seconds I actually had was long enough to see who was there besides the three remaining insurgents – a pilot and a technician who worked the winches with the grappling cables – and to figure out where I thought they were from by the control labels of the craft.

A sign on the corner, white on red, said "CAUTION! Warm Engine Slowly." But what it actually said was "УВАГА! Тепла Двигун Повільно," which was a different thing altogether. Barely, I knew that much Ukrainian.

I caught a glimpse of a couple of push buttons near the dials. One said "Вступати" – Engage. Another read "Вбити." You pronounced that "vbyty" and it meant Kill. This was a fully equipped military operation. The coffin was strapped loosely to the inner hull with bungees. What did these guys want with Jack's body?

That was what I wondered when I spun instinctively to slam an elbow into the face of the black jump-suited man behind me who had the butt of an AR-15 poised to collide with my skull.

I found this convenient.

I took advantage of his momentary shock to grab the weapon from the man's hands, kick him to the deck and holler "Hey there!" at the other four – the pilot, the technician and two more grapplers in black.

Could've been any of a dozen things I did wrong to make the guy I hit realize I wasn't one of them – the way I stood, the tight fit of my appropriated clothes, a signal I had missed, didn't matter. If nothing else, the yarmulke still bobby-pinned to my hair gave me away. A few rounds from the AR-15 through the windshield of the Huey got the other guys' attention.

In Ukrainian I demanded that they put the craft down. "Va-nizz," I said and I was sure I said it right. But they looked at each other, tentatively, as though they had no idea what I was saying.

It was virtually the same word in Russian. So I tried "Pastga" – which meant "down" in Uzbek. No dice. "Z'minn," Lithuanian. "Jos," Romanian. "Dolu," Czech. I was running out of eastern European languages.

"Just get this thing down, dammit!" I said.

The pilot held up an open hand. "You want to land," he said, "okay."

They turned out to be American – or at least the pilot was. Probably the others were too. So why the Ukrainian insignia? Was it to throw me off? They didn't even know I was coming. We were above a rocky area but there was a smooth platform of rock at the top of a small peak. The pilot seemed to hesitate, to hover. I still had the submachine gun dangling at the end of my left arm. The engineer was still on the deck but one of the commandos made a quick move in my direction.

I blocked him with a knee and spun with the weapon to shoot through the front right cabin wall and put a clean hole in the fuel tank. The petroleum leak was visible on the dropping fuel gauge.

"Feel more like landing now, pal?" I asked the pilot. "Right there. You see it. It's stable enough. I'd do it myself but I'm busy keeping your friends off the merchandise."

He was a good pilot. He put the runners down on a flat rock barely wide enough to hold them.

"Now you tell me. You – in the jump suit," I was talking to the only remaining crew member with whom I hadn't had an argument yet. "What do you guys want with this coffin? You know it's already occupied, right?"

He shrugged. "Don't know," he said.

"Where are you taking it?"

He shrugged again.

I swept the back of my free hand across his face and asked the same question of the man leaning against the hull next to him. I kicked the back of the pilot's seat – hard – and said "Where?"

"Ouch!" he said. "Not a clue. I was going to get instructions en route."

He would probably not get those instructions by the 'copter's radio, I realized. That could have been on a trackable public band. I demanded their cell phones and they hesitated enough in surrendering them that I knew they at least wished they could keep them. I made the four of them leave the helicopter and walk – they had no idea where. We were in a barren area at the northern edge of Los Angeles surrounded by small mountains and woods. That was Rocky Peak to the north and El Escorpion to the east. I had run and biked these trails for more than twenty years now. I knew my way around here but I doubted these guys would.

They would climb down from our landing platform and come across a well worn hiking trail. Probably no one would be out on a weekday afternoon to tell them where to go. They'd walk the right way or the wrong way. In either case it would be easy enough for the police to pick them up.

I had the Huey in the air before the four of them climbed down the hill.

It drove me crazy how long it took a 911 operator to answer. This time my cell rang for twelve minutes before I got a response. I had time to figure out where I was going. A hospital nearby had a helipad on the roof of the emergency department but if a second craft tried to land with a real emergency while I was there I could cause a problem. The place to go was the municipal helispot near the police dispatch center. Nine landing sites, no waiting. I banked to the east. I had enough fuel left in my leaking tank to leapfrog over El Escorpion but I'd better not try anything any fancier than that.

"State the nature of your emergency," the female voice from my phone said, finally.

"Four felons lately involved in a possible intelligence operation involving a stolen cadaver in eastern Ventura County," I said. "They're fleeing on foot in the vicinity of the Cave of Munits."

"Cave of ... what? I'm sorry, who is this?"

"Munits. Cave of Munits. Look it up on a road map. It's heavily wooded. Tell the boys to bring a couple of four-wheelers and maybe a skidder." I gave her my rank and serial number. She would look that up too and it would freak her out royally.

"Excuse me, sir. Your name was —" and I flipped the phone off. She had her information. It rang again a few seconds later but I ignored it. I had to land.

Three police officers stood on the helispot as I hovered above it. One pulled out a radio and soon more policemen would file out of a building at the edge of the helispot. Then the 'copter radio paged me. I hovered some more.

I flipped a switch and a scratchy voice said, "Jacks over jaguars."

Of course, I realized. There would be no call over the guys' cell phones. The radio used unconventional bands. That was the point of using the Ukrainian equipment. It might even be untraceable. Oh well, at least our body thieves wouldn't be able to call for help from the hiking trail.

"Jacks over jaguars," the radio said again. I flipped a switch.

"Yeah, what's my destination?" I said.

"Jacks over jaguars."

"Can't be bothered. Destination."

"I need a countersign."

"I'm sure you do. Look I've had a long day and it's not even two in the afternoon. Where are we taking the stiff?"

"Am I to understand that you –"

"You guys failed to anticipate any adversity. We're down a man and another's got a punctured lung. We're all banged up, barely got the cargo intact. Just tell me where I can drop this box off and get a shower and find a doc and maybe we won't knock your head off when we get there."

The line went dead, but just for a moment.

A different voice came on the wire and said, "Santa Monica Airport. Southwest corner of Barker Hangar," and the radio went dead, for good this time.

Below me somewhere between a dozen and twenty Los Angeles city police congregated on the helispot. I dropped a few feet out of my hover and they cleared a landing pad. They all had cuffs or weapons out as I touched down.

I waved both hands outside the cab before I showed my face. After a moment I edged slowly around my open hatch to stand with my back to them and my hands flat on the hull. They pulled my hands back one at a time and cuffed them together.

Now what should I tell them first, I wondered. Who I was or what I've got aboard the helicopter?

There wasn't a square foot on the European continent in 1944 that was reliably isolated enough for us to parachute in without detection. From the Black Forest at the southern tip of Germany to the mountainous wasteland surrounding the little principality of Andorra, access to every spot of ground on the continent was arguably watched by someone. If we dropped into enemy territory German forces could see us and take us prisoner at any time. If we dropped into Italy or some other spot in Allied hands we would still have to fight through the front lines. If we went in through some neutral zone like Switzerland or even Belgium – both in enemy control at the time – there'd be hell to pay in Washington; there'd be painstaking reevaluation of alliances and agreements. There wasn't any hand-to-hand in DC, but there was a war on at home too. The most practical means of entry was to mix in with the invasion force.

We crossed the channel in these flat motorized boats with a couple dozen guys huddled on each one. D-Day was on a Tuesday. Osprey and I landed with the wave that came in the following Thursday.

"What did you mean 'gone'?" I finally got around to asking Osprey as the flat bottom of our boat clapped over and over again against the choppy surface of the English Channel.

"Whaddya mean whaddimean 'gone'?"

"When I saw you sitting at the boss's anteroom before Donovan hustled me in the office. 'Gone,' you said when I asked about the Old Doc. What did he quit or defect or –"

"Dead," Osprey said.

"Dead how?" I wanted to know.

"Ambushed. Probably fifth column guys or something. I left a few bullet wounds behind but I barely got out alive."

"What? Why? He was a scientist not a soldier."

"Lookin' for the secret formula, I expect."

"He had a secret formula for …"

"You. They wanted to get their hands on what made you into," he looked me up and down, "this."

"How'd they know?"

"Know what? About you?"

"I'm a big secret."

"You're running around Italy and the eastern front all spectacular and stuff. And was that you who pulled off that aircraft carrier thing off the coast of Singapore a few months back? How many times you been around the world in the last two years?"

"Lost count."

"I bet you did. And they're giving Doolittle and Monty all the credit for air superiority in Europe but that was you in that P-57 a few months back. Right? The one that dropped upside-down in a flat spin and pulled up the last moment no higher above the ground than the top of a phone pole? Whuzzat you, Steve?"

"Just showing them this idea I had. Now you've got whole units of dive bombers doing stuff like that like a dance company. Those Air Corps guys are amazing."

"The ones that make it out alive, yeah. You know the Krauts have got to know about you. They're not idiots. Hell, I bet even the Russians know."

"Even the Russians? They're not idiots either."

"Really? Have you met Stalin?"

"No," I said, "I haven't."

"I have," Osprey said.

"Really? How?"

"I get around a little too. Old Joe ain't someone you want splashing around your hereditary swamp if y'know what I mean."

I had to give Osprey credit. We were out of sight of either the British or French coast and the channel surface was white with froth. Most of the guys in the craft hung over the rail surrendering their breakfast. It didn't seem to faze Osprey.

"So did they get the formula? The super-soldier formula?"

"Hell no," Osprey said.

"Well the government must have it. The War Department?"

"They don't. Why d'ya think they only made one of you?"

"Are you sure they didn't get it? The Jerries I mean?"

Osprey was quiet for a moment. Then, "Yeah I'm sure. You'll be alone in the world for a while, Steve."

I thought about that when Osprey pointed off the bow of the boat – or whatever this heap was.

"Is that?" Osprey asked and trailed off. "Yeah, land ho," he said softly and pointed at the horizon toward a wide shadow. There it was, the coast of France, just like that. "Will you excuse me a second, Captain?"

And finally Osprey leaned off the starboard side and spent the next minute-and-a-half unloading most of his meals of the past several days.

Casualties on Omaha Beach were north of seventy percent. My priority was to protect Osprey and get him to a labor camp southwest of Hechingen, the town where I was to meet Dr Heisenberg and infiltrate the Germans' big bomb program. What with the makeshift barriers the Germans had set up underwater all along the coast – batteries of long pointed sticks, makeshift sandbars and the like – the boats could not get closer than fifty or a hundred feet from shore. During the previous weeks the Air Force tried to bomb out those barriers and instead planted deep underwater gullies along the way. Men carrying weapons and sixty-pound packs who happened into one of those concussion gullies dropped out of sight, never to be seen again. Osprey was more concerned with random bullet spray from the land than with holes underwater. Twice I yanked him back when he was about to step in one when I could see a discoloration of the water above it.

On the beach the gunfire was sporadic. We were wading into an extended battle now in its third day. The Nazis had known we were coming but they had no idea where or when. They probably had air photos of troops massing and these barges full of men accumulating across the channel. They peppered the French coast with bunkers that held marksmen inside. They met the landing in Normandy with horrific violence and death.

The wall of German snipers got more porous for the two miles between the beach and the first road we came upon. Gunfire was mostly in the distance now so we followed the road as best we could. It had been paved once. Now it was pockmarked with small arms marks and frequent craters. In some places where there had been an explosion we couldn't see where the lost road continued. In those cases I would look out to where the undergrowth seemed sparser and we would find traces of a path and maybe some asphalt or a layer of gravel until a road appeared again.

We found an abandoned Italian personnel carrier by the side of the road. It had a bed like a pickup truck, but wider, and room for the driver and one or two other passengers up front. What an Italian vehicle was doing in northern France two years after the fall of Mussolini I'll never know. All it needed, Osprey told me, were an alternator and some engine wires. In the next couple of abandoned vehicles we came across, we found some parts. Osprey could rig up the carrier with that. We siphoned whatever gas there was from every empty vehicle this former road had claimed. Some of the cars and tanks along the way still contained traces – limbs, a few mostly intact bodies – of their sometime passengers.

We slept in random barns and haylofts along the way, and a couple of times when we found sufficient cover we slept in our vehicle. We ran into significant adversity in the form of Axis troops in a few places. Somewhere in Alsace we took fire from what turned out to be a platoon of Brits who landed a day before we had. Osprey and I were separated twice. I found him both times.

We reached the environs of the desolate ancient village of Hechingen the day of the summer solstice. Now came the hard part.

The beans were spilled. The news was broke. The bag was cat-free. There was no pretending any more that the feds didn't know where I was or who I was claiming to be. The moment I showed the coffin in the Huey to the Los Angeles police I was identified as the captain again. Thousand Oaks was nice while it lasted.

"Please let your supervisors know that they need to dispatch a team to the Santa Monica airport, Barker Hangar. The southwest corner," I said before they had the cuffs off me.

"What kind of team?" an officer asked.

"An armed and dangerous one," I said, "and it would be a good idea to investigate the contiguous buildings and the access points to the hangar as well before they crash in loaded for bear."

"What are you –"

"Not sure yet. But somebody needs to be there soon. Just get the word up the line, please. Barker Hangar."

I helped the officers load the coffin onto a dolly and we wheeled it into a garage. It was ten past three when I sat in the radio room of the police barracks by the helispot among several taciturn, suspicious police officers. It was three-thirty-five when the radio operator turned and said that an Air Force team would arrive in the next few minutes.

We all went back outside to the landing area and waited for my ride to touch down.

✪   ✪   ✪

Osprey and I were alone, deep in enemy territory. Ultimately I left him near the entrance to the work camp outside the Hechingen town limits where we saw the company of men filing out in the morning like the world's most pitiful chain gang. I didn't want to leave him there, but I did. It was his mission and he insisted.

"Here help me with this here, Steve." Osprey hunched over the creased hull of an abandoned truck that sat aside the road running by the entrance to the work camp less than a quarter-mile away. Osprey had his shirt off and was trying to catch a piece of the shirt's chest on a jagged dent in the truck fender.

"What are you doing?"

"I'm trying to tear a strip of the shirt down the side."

"It's a perfectly good shirt. A little ratty just now but all it needs is a good washing."

"That's the problem," Osprey said. "Did you see those guys who left here just now? You see what they looked like?"

The gang of about forty men, disheveled and despairing, filed out the entrance of the walled-in camp about twenty minutes earlier, overseen by four crisp, ramrod-straight German officers. The men from the camp were uniformly emaciated and miserable looking as they trudged, long knotted ropes tying them together at the ankles like a company of circus elephants. They had gone up the road toward the village and disappeared over a rise.

"See their clothes? Not a one of 'em had his clothes intact. Shirts like rags. Pants like loincloths. See that kid couldn't have been more than fourteen all bare-backed in this sun? Practically naked. Talk about dehumanizing."

"Yeah, I saw."

"Bad enough I look pretty well fed even after a couple weeks on the road. I gotta blend in. Gotta mix. Gotta mingle."

"If that's what you've got to do," I said, taking the shirt from him. "Wish I knew why you're going in that hell hole at all."

"'Cuz I can pass for Jewish."

"It's not safe. Wish I knew what your mission was. I could help, you know."

Osprey grunted.

I got a thumb in a tiny hole Osprey had poked in the shirt and I drew the tear down to the seam. "How's that?"

"Good start," Osprey said and ripped at it some more.

Not long before dusk the company of bound residents of the work camp along with their Nazi overlords returned from up the road. It seemed there were fewer of them now, but I hadn't counted them when they left.

"Time for you to make yourself scarce now Steve," Osprey was darkly tanned from our days on the road. Then he slouched in his torn clothing and suddenly he inhabited a new identity, like a gifted actor. He looked for all the world like a lost soul. Strangely softly, he said, "In eight days at eleven p.m. By that string of rocks by the town limits sign. Unless I signal before that. Right?"

"I'll be there."

He walked along through a wooded area beside the road and, before he was able to blend in with the group a German officer spotted him and ordered him to get back with the group. If anyone wondered why he was not wearing a rope on his ankle it seemed no one cared to ask.

Now I had eight days and a few hours to get my own job done.

✪   ✪   ✪

The LAPD recovered Jack's body and took the would-be commandos into custody before I got to Santa Monica. Who were they and why in the world would they want to steal Jack's body? They turned out to be a collection of itinerant freelance button men, a little desperate in the contemporary economy, that the agents of some overseas information traders put together on the fly. I suppose I should have insisted on questioning them, but it was clear to the police that they knew very little.

I convinced the LAPD officers that the only way get the erstwhile commandoes' contacts to identify themselves was to have the big Huey roll into the hangar at roughly the time they expected it. Before that happened, half a dozen Los Angeles plainclothesmen walked in posing as mechanics, flight crew members and one guy as a potential buyer of a used Gulfstream. Two women and a man perched in separate corners of the hangar, waiting, when technicians drove the wide trailer on which I had touched down the runners of my black Huey.

One of my contacts dropped to the floor from a scaffolding structure along one wall that looked like a big erector set, and another from the saddle of a fork lift at a far corner. The third, with a heavy tool belt around his waist, dropped the handle of a broom on the hangar floor near me and all three walked toward the helicopter. All three moved with their left arms swinging and their right hands hovering by side pockets, the walking posture of people accustomed to carrying a weapon. All three probably were.

I crouched inside by the crew door, pulled down the handle so I could yank it back on its rollers and a bullet cracked through the door window above my head. They didn't waste time. Probably we had saved the lives of the commandoes and crew who had stolen Jack's body when we arrested them.

"Hold it there," the voice came from about forty feet away. "Drop your weapons and let me see your –"

– and the one who had shot through the window wheeled around with her handgun, took a policeman's bullet to her left lower abdomen and dropped on the ground.

The other two raised their hands and went to their knees. The plainclothesmen were gathered around the three of them when I hopped down from the 'copter's open crew door. The police were cuffing all three of them, including the wounded woman.

As I hit the ground I said, "Excuse me," and took a large wrench out of the tool belt of the handcuffed man.

"We're all a little disappointed we didn't get to see you in action, Cap," one of the plainclothes officers said …

… as I spun to launch the wrench in the direction of the driver of the helicopter trailer and shouldered one of the LA cops to shove him out of the path of the driver's bullet.

The wrench hit home in the driver's gut and I wasn't far behind it.

I ran toward him, my first step on hands and knees and the next three strides brought me in a horizontal leap at the driver. I wrapped his waist in my right arm and grabbed his pistol wrist with my left hand and he tumbled backward with me still holding on.

I rolled off him to my left and snatched up his gun from the floor where it landed. I held it in the air by its warm muzzle.

"Everyone in the room is either a witness or a suspect," I said loudly enough to reach all the corners of the big hangar.

It's not like I had to attract anyone's attention. The two gunshots of the past twenty seconds had already done that.

As it became clear that the last of the gun-toters was cuffed and disarmed fifteen people – custodians, mechanics, random passengers and a couple of pilots – emerged from cover and gave the policemen their names and contact numbers.

Then I went home.

✪　　✪　　✪

Werner Heisenberg was a formidable guy. I knew that twelve years earlier, in 1932 at the age of thirty, he won the Nobel Prize in physics. When Einstein won his he had been in his forties. I managed to connect with Heisenberg in a little beer garden in Hechingen the night I first got into town. I thought that even for German government operatives the group of four men among whom Heisenberg sat sipping from a mug, were quiet and reserved.

I ordered something non-alcoholic but which could pass for a cocktail – tonic water with bitters – slugged it down on a bar stool and ordered another. Then I got up, waved at nobody across the room and made my way past where Heisenberg sat, making a point of tripping over the heavy coat draped over the back of Heisenberg's chair.

I sprawled over the floor impressively, I thought.

Nobody made a move. I thought they were going to ignore me. Okay, what do I do now, I wanted to know. Should I roll over and grab my ankle and moan in pain? Or should I slam my elbow through a leg of one of their chairs? Or I should get up and walk quietly out the door? Or something?

I rolled onto my back and over me stood the youngest of Heisenberg's party with an arm out for me to grab. It was Kurt Diebner who, I later learned, was the German government's man on the scene, the Reich's overseer of what they called the Uranverein – the Uranium Club. I was quite a bit larger than Diebner but I pretended to struggle to my feet as I grasped his forearm and flexed my thighs to get upright. I affected a limp for the time I was there.

"Danke," I said to Diebner and continued in German. "May I buy all of you gentlemen a beer?" Actually, may I you gentlemen a beer buy? My biggest problem with German – besides the accent – was figuring out how to migrate the verb to the end of the sentence.

But I must have done it correctly because it earned me a seat at the table.

I was Peter Bossert, a research fellow at the hospital in Haigerloch, I told them. I was working on a project that had to do with detecting problems in the digestive tract by feeding a patient small amounts of radioactive material. I was making it all up, but I thought the radioactivity connection might pique these physicists' interest. Mostly I wanted to strike up a conversation with Heisenberg, who sat impassively sucking on a little white clay pipe even when a waitress put a fresh stein of beer in front of him.

"You do these procedures on humans?" Diebner wanted to know.

"No, not yet." I said.

"On what then?" another of the physicists asked.

"Rats mostly," I said. "Dogs sometimes."

"And they live?"

"Actually no," I said, "not yet. Sometimes they last long enough to expel the trace substance."

"What do you use?" Diebner asked. "What substance?"

"Radium," I said. "The problem is getting the dose small enough to avoid poisoning the patient but large enough to track. It's a conundrum." I used the word "rätsel" – a mystery or a puzzle.

"Radium. Interesting," Dr Heisenberg said. It was the first time he spoke up.

"Dogs and rats?" Diebner said.

"Yes."

"You should take advantage of the fact that you are in Germany and requisition some Jews," Diebner the problem-solver suggested.

"Jews?"

"As test subjects," another of the scientists said. "They are much closer to human anatomy than dogs are."

This conversation was taking a disturbing turn.

"I would be glad to submit the necessary forms for you, Herr Bossert," Diebner said. "We can acquire the subjects from the work camp right here at the edge of town. Would a pair of adult males be sufficient?"

"I would have to clear that with my biochemistry advisor," I said. "That would change the parameters of the study." Considering how seldom I spoke German I was very proud of using the word prämisse – a theory or a basis for an idea – and for knowing it in the first place.

I was less proud of myself when, as the company of scientists and I left the tavern, Dr Heisenberg took me by the arm and urged me to walk with him in a direction away from the others. "Say 'radium,' would you?" Heisenberg said.

"Radium," I said with my best rolled 'R.'

"And 'prämisse?'" he said.

"Prämisse," I said, with a less pronounced 'R' this time.

"You're rolling your 'R's' like a Frenchman with your tongue on the roof of your mouth," Heisenberg told me. "In German you do it back in your throat." He demonstrated. "Rrrrrr. It's heavier."

"Rrrrrr," I tried.

"Better," Heisenberg said, "even a French Swiss would know that." He turned down the next corner, said, "We talk tomorrow," and melted into the night.

✪　　✪　　✪

"What can I do?" I wanted to know.

"Come eat. We have plenty of food." Jonathan's voice was raspy over the phone, like his grandfather's. Jonathan was a student at UCLA working on a master's degree in architecture and urban design. Bright boy. He combed his dusty blond hair straight back over his head the way Jack had, and he even affected a little hitch in his walk. I had never realized before how much like his grandfather he was. "Feel like helping me identify Grampa's body?"

"Oh. Damn. I'll be right there," and I offered to drive.

They didn't let people into the actual morgue at Los Robles Hospital. Surgeons conducted autopsies and harvested organs in the same big room as the walls full of cold storage drawers. Jonathan and I stood in a hall where an orderly wheeled a gurney to us.

Jonathan put a hand on the wall for a moment and seemed about to lose his composure. I reached a hand toward his shoulder but he waved it away. He was fine until the drive back home. Jack looked a lot more peaceful than he had at the airport, but I didn't bring that up.

I noticed a discoloration on his left side behind his arm, and I remembered. "Is that a tattoo?" I asked Jonathan.

"A tattoo. Yeah. I think it was a war thing."

"A war thing," I said. I had seen a war thing like that only once before. There were no words or insignia. It was just a circle of thirty-two smaller circles, with one of them filled in.

We confirmed to the attendant at the morgue that the body was indeed Jack's. In the car on the way back it was Jonathan who brought up the tattoo again.

"Gramma said he brought it back from the war with him," Jonathan said. "He never talked about it if anyone ever noticed or asked him about it. I asked him when I was little and we were in the pool once."

"Did he tell you not to ask him about it?"

"No, he just said when I was older. Said he might tell me when I was older."

"And did he?"

"No," Jonathan said, and then, "maybe."

"Uh-huh? What'd he say?"

"He said it was a treasure map. I think he was talking about the tattoo. Maybe not."

"You think he was? When did he tell you?"

"At somebody's wedding. Or maybe it was a bar mitzvah. I'm not sure. I must have been sixteen or seventeen because I think I was still in high school. Yeah, I was seventeen. It must have been my cousin Dave's bar mitzvah. It was my last year of high school."

"And he just told you that?"

"Yeah. He was sitting with his friend Joe from work joking about something, waving an empty glass in the air. So he gets up and sees me and he grabs me around the collar and drags me away from my friends over to the bar. He says, 'Have you got a good taste for wine?' and I told him not really. So he hands the bartender the empty glass and Grampa asks me if I'm twenty-one yet. Like I should tell him I'm twenty-one if I want a drink, but I said, 'I'm seventeen, Grampa.' And the bartender gives him a fishy look and Grampa gets me a Sprite and a bourbon for himself."

"Jack was a bourbon man? I didn't know that."

"I don't think so. He just really liked weddings and bar mitzvahs," Jonathan said. "Hated funerals. I don't like them much either."

"Yeah me neither," I said.

"So he says, 'You're a good kid, Jonny.' He only called me Jonny at weddings and bar mitzvahs, it seemed. And he said, 'Know that thing under my arm?' and I wasn't sure what he meant because I didn't even remember the tattoo, but it must have been the tattoo, right?"

"I guess."

"'It's a treasure map,' Grampa says. 'I been walking around with a treasure map since before your dad was born. Hah!' He said 'Hah!' just like that. Not like he was laughing. Just 'Hah!' he said."

"Hah!" I said. "What else did he tell you?"

"Nothing. He sat down with Joe again and right away they both started laughing again and I went and tried to dance with my cousin. I'm not much of a dancer but neither is she."

"Me neither," I said but that was a lie. I do a mean Lindy Hop.

That was what it was, though. I knew it now. It was a treasure map. I dropped Jonathan off at his grandmother's house all crowded with family, made my excuses and headed back to the morgue.

✪   ✪   ✪

In Hechingen I stayed in a guest house that was owned by a dour thin man who looked to be in his forties, and a jolly round woman apparently in her sixties. I never heard their names other than as a mumble and I never figured out their relationship. I liked to think she was his mother but I suppose she might not have been. Around six-thirty that last night I answered a knock on my door and found Werner Heisenberg stranding by the stairs.

"Come on in, Dr Heisenberg," I said, and he did.

"I brought some papers for you, Mr Bossert," Heisenberg said. He pulled a small sheaf of yellow printed forms out of his inner jacket pocket. "Requisition forms," he said.

"You're requisitioning something from me?"

"For you. Diebner was going to bring these himself but I suggested it was a better idea for me to drop them by."

On the top line of the first page it said, "leben spezifische zuweisung." Live specimen allocation. Oh Lord he wanted me to commandeer some Jews to experiment on.

"You should fill out the forms and sign them, Peter."

"I should?"

"Diebner is the government contact with our group. With the Uranium Club. Helping you with your research in this way was his idea."

"He's your government oversight guy? Diebner is?"

"He is. He's not a scientist. He was a high school science teacher. I have spent a good portion of the past few years leading him to think I believe his ideas are all good ones. It would be to your advantage to let him think that you think this is a fine idea too."

I took the papers, put them on a small night table and asked Heisenberg if he would like to go up the street for a beer. He thought it might be more prudent for us to stay in, and he retrieved a bag of beer bottles he had placed on the floor outside my door before he knocked on it.

"You are either a British intelligence operative trying to determine how far along our little operation has gotten," Heisenberg said after consuming about half of his first liter, "or an aspiring young journalist looking for a reputation."

I smiled. I think that for a moment my smile actually scared him. "Which would you rather I would be, Dr Heisenberg?"

"For your sake or mine, Mr Bossert?"

We danced around that idea for a while, and when I was satisfied that it was safe enough I brought up the Uranium Club. Heisenberg did indeed know a lot about atomic fission that was in no textbook. It seemed he occupied most of his work time coming up with elaborate tests that would both waste a maximum amount of the club's resources and keep their usable supply of fissile material well below any critical mass.

Besides protecting Osprey, my mission was to find out what Heisenberg knew about building an atomic bomb. I never really found out what he knew, but it was clear to me that whatever it was, he wasn't telling anyone – least of all the German government authorities. At four o'clock, the morning after that evening when I had my last conversation with Heisenberg, the flare out my guest room window rose silently into the sky. Osprey needed me.

I got into the hospital in Los Robles through the emergency entrance with a story about having dropped off a friend in ortho earlier in the day. I made my way to the basement morgue and got into the big room with a toothpick and a Swiss Army knife. The first thing I noticed was the breeze coming from the open window high on a far wall. The second was that there was already a body lying out on the gurney in the middle of the room. There was someone here.

I had already made enough noise coming in to be sure whoever was here was already aware of me. I slid into a shadow between the door and a big trash can. I did not have to wait long before Jack's visitor – and if there was only one of them there would be another waiting outside the open window – gave away his position. As I floated my hand toward the cover of the trash can there was a shuffling from behind the gurney.

The moment I was sure of the intruder's position crouching behind the gurney I swept up the cover of the trash can with my right hand and clapped my left palm onto a lab table in front of me. I threw my legs into the air and pivoted on my left hand to get as much height as I could and flung the trash cover at the guy like a frisbee.

Plastic. It was all I had.

It stunned him enough. I was on him like a barnacle.

He was a slight, thin guy wearing a loose long-sleeve polo shirt. I tied him to a heavy piece of equipment with an electric wire, ripped the sleeves off his shirt and slid them over my arms.

I stuck my arms with the sleeves over them out the open window and the guy's confederate took my hands to pull me out. I yanked downward and pulled him halfway through the narrow window.

He didn't fit, but so much the better. I put him out and tied him awkwardly with another wire to the faucets in a fixed-position lab table so he wouldn't be able to get down even if he woke up soon.

As I expected, the body on the gurney was Jack's. I checked again on his tattooed diagram and found the item it pointed out.

To be safe, rather than return Jack's body to a drawer and risk mistaken identity, I left him out on the gurney and my two intruders tied and unconscious nearby. On a wall there was a phone which I picked up and dialed 9-1-1. I identified myself to the emergency dispatcher who eventually answered, told her where the police could find the mess I left behind and got out of the building the way I came in.

Now, what to do with what I found here?

No one had ever questioned my possession of the old Italian personnel carrier I was still using to roll around Hechingen. It seemed there was a war on. Well before I reached the work camp at the southern edge of town I could see the fires climb above the shadows of the buildings. The chaos, the people running every which-way in the streets, reached me before I got within sight of the work camp. I had to hit my brakes three or four times in the course of the last few hundred yards. One of those times Osprey appeared at the passenger door, flung it open and scrambled in.

"How's your night vision?" was the first thing he said.

"Pretty good," I said. "Nice seeing you again too."

He wore the same tattered shirt and shoes I left him in, a little worse for wear. It looked as though he had found a pair of shorts and he carried a bulky satchel. "Kill the headlights," he said, and as soon as I did I heard sirens from somewhere behind us. "Menachem!" Osprey hollered out the window, "In back!" and I felt someone clatter into the bed of the vehicle.

And then the carrier thumped several more times. More passengers.

"That's all that's comin', Steve. Let's go."

"Tell them to keep their heads down," and I hit the gas.

The last lit-up thing I saw that night was the gate of the work camp, dressed in flames up to the sky. I got the vehicle onto the darkest, narrowest country roads I could find before the sirens got any closer and we all vanished into the night, with the pedal crowding the floor all the way.

The carrier did not have a working fuel indicator so I put gasoline in the thing every chance I had. We stopped twice that first night to siphon gas out of trucks we found along the way. When the sun started creeping over the edge of the Earth, Osprey and I decided it was time to find somewhere to hide from the daylight.

"Plenty of abandoned houses along here," Osprey said. "Let's find one. Somewhere that looks like there haven't been any repairs in a while."

"How do we know it's abandoned?"

"You and I go in first, and if it isn't abandoned we'll be the only ones who know. These guys have to stay safe. Try to find one with a power cable running into it."

As it got light I stopped at a little country cottage quite a distance from its closest neighbors. It had been a lovely place once. Shingles missing from the roof were scattered in front. A broken bulb hung from a single porch lamp without a cover. Torn dolls and a dead soccer ball and such lay scattered behind a tattered picket fence. I certainly hoped it was abandoned.

Osprey and I got out and I saw for the first time that there were eleven men, ranging in age from mid-teens to about fifty, huddled in the back of the personnel carrier. All but the young boys looked in worse shape than Osprey, and those kids didn't look wonderful either. We scoped out the house and – I was thankful – found it empty. The power was out but Osprey was excited that he found a generator in back.

"Would you go get the guys and make sure they have a place to roost?" he asked me. "I'll be out back."

"Will do," I said. It seemed to me that I had a rather crucial mission here, to monitor the major players in Germany's atomics program. Osprey was taking his own mission – and specifically what was its objective I never really learned – very seriously as well. By now I had determined that my own mission was complete, so now I was essentially an operative of Osprey's project, whatever it was.

From what I could determine, one of these eleven guys I was emptying out the back of the truck was very valuable to someone stateside for some reason. I never did find out why or even who it was, but the other ten were along for the ride. They were all the guys from the work camp whom Osprey was able to save and now it was our job to find safety for them.

I got everyone indoors with somewhere to sleep if they could manage it, and I found Osprey behind the cottage messing around with what looked like an alien ray gun plugged into the electric generator.

"Hey Steve," Osprey called when he saw me. "Help me with this thing, would you?"

"What is it?" I had no idea.

"Art equipment," he said. "Here," and he handed me a slip of paper from the satchel with a pencil design on it.

It was a pattern of thirty-two circles, arranged in an oval – sixteen above and sixteen below. One of the circles on the lower part of the oval arrangement was filled in, and all the others were open circles.

"It's the tattoo gizmo from the death camp. They put a number on all their prisoners' forearms with it, so I swiped it. I need to put a tattoo like this on me somewhere." He handed me the ink gun and pulled up the left side of his shirt. "Here, Steve. You do it, would you?"

"Me? What kind of pattern is this?"

"Call it a war souvenir. Just a bunch of circles laid out in a circle. Go ahead."

I hesitated, but I hefted the gun in both hands and tried to guide the tip of the needle to feed the pattern of a circle onto Osprey's side under his left arm. It was not particularly heavy for me, but the lines of what was supposed to be a circle came out jagged and uneven.

"Ah, now look what you did," Osprey was disappointed. "Hand me that, hey?"

"Sorry."

"No problem. I'll just make that the lower bicuspid." Then with the artistic confidence that soon would make him a fine career in civilian life, he grabbed a handful of his own hair with his left hand and with his right hand he used the ink gun to turn my irregular shape into a small darkened-in circle.

It was not a particularly pleasant thing to watch, but it seemed as though the operation should have been awkward so I sat and watched Osprey to make sure he didn't drop his tool or get hurt. He didn't do either, but after a few minutes he had a perfectly drawn circle of thirty-two circles under his arm, with one filled in.

Over the next several weeks, avoiding conflict against both Osprey's and my instincts, we made our way through the contentious countryside between Hechingen and the coast. We managed not to lose anyone and to latch onto a roadload of tanks full of British Desert Rats, fresh from liberating the city of Ghent.

They brought us to a company of Canadian soldiers who got us to Bruges. There, the thirteen of us picked up a cargo transport across the channel to Dover and safety, such as it is.

✪   ✪   ✪

I stood in my living room in Thousand Oaks and contemplated what I had taken from the morgue. In the hearth was an armful of aged maple, simmering away. I wondered whether this was the last time I would be able to enjoy the fireplace in this comfortable little home. Soon – I didn't know how soon – duty would take me away from this place. On my coffee table was what appeared to be a tooth – a lower-right bicuspid. It was made of gold and porcelain and was apparently an early iteration of an implant. It had a screw attachment that had been bored into Jack's lower jaw. I wondered what was inside.

I got a hammer and a tweezer from the toolbox in my laundry room, put the false tooth on the wooden floor and smashed the tooth open. I pried off the gold shell and found a metallic cube that appeared to be solid. As it happens, it was solid. On the surfaces, though, were tiny embossed letters. It must have been hundredth-of-a-point type, paragraphloads of lettering.

I didn't even have a pair of reading glasses around. I found a magnifying glass from an old Halloween costume and, with my stepped-up vision, that was good enough for me to see what the information on the cube was.

These were the detailed instructions from Osprey's – Jack's – late employer the Old Doc, on how to create what they had made of me. There were chemical formulas, how-to descriptions of machinery, supply sources, detailed procedures on how to create a super-soldier. There was even a rudimentary budget. Extrapolating into today's money, it would probably cost a government about three or four million dollars per enlistee. I realized that, given what Jack had told me all those years ago, this was almost certainly the sole recorded account of how to do this.

Outside in my driveway a few cars pulled up. Two of them had flashing lights on them. They were military vehicles. My cell phone rang.

"Yes, I'm inside," I told the voice on the other end. "Give me a moment. I'll be right out."

I picked up the pieces of the tooth implant and the cube with the information written in tiny type, looked at them in my palm, then tossed it all into the flames. I put the safety screen in front of the fireplace and let it continue to burn.

From behind the dryer in the laundry room I scooped up the big round shield – much more effective than the plastic trash can cover, I noted – and went out the front door, wondering what would happen next.

Sometime toward the beginning of November of 1944 I reported to President Roosevelt and General Wild Bill Donovan that the best way to undermine the German atomic weapons development program – the Uranium Club – was to make sure Werner Heisenberg remained in charge of it.

I hoped the Americans had a scientist of comparable integrity at the helm of the Manhattan Project.

ALSO BY ELLIOT S! MAGGIN

SUPERMAN: LAST SON OF KRYPTON

SUPERMAN: MIRACLE MONDAY

GENERATION X (WITH SCOTT LOBDELL)

KINGDOM COME (BASED ON THE COMIC BOOK SERIES
BY MARK WAID AND ALEX ROSS)

NOT MY CLOSET

Elliot S! Maggin has been making up stories as long as he can remember. He started publishing them when he was 17. He made his living writing comic books for a long time, including a 15-year run as principal writer of Superman for DC Comics. He was educated at Brandeis and Columbia Universities and his best accomplishments are his two ridiculously talented adult children. He has written journalism, novels, television and film for lots of publishers and producers. He likes fiction best.

Be in touch:

http://Elliot.Maggin.com

Made in the USA
Middletown, DE
20 September 2017